W9-AQL-742

06/2021

Dear Parents:

Congratulations! Your child is taking
the first steps on an exciting journey.
The destination? Independent reading!

STEP INTO READING® will help your child get there. The program offers
five steps to reading success. Each step includes fun stories and colorful
art or photographs. In addition to original fiction and books with favorite
characters, there are Step into Reading Non-Fiction Readers, Phonics Readers
and Boxed Sets, Sticker Readers, and Comic Readers—a complete literacy
program with something to interest every child.

Learning to Read, Step by Step!

Ready to Read   Preschool–Kindergarten
• big type and easy words • rhyme and rhythm • picture clues
For children who know the alphabet and are eager to
begin reading.

Reading with Help   Preschool–Grade 1
• basic vocabulary • short sentences • simple stories
For children who recognize familiar words and sound out
new words with help.

Reading on Your Own   Grades 1–3
• engaging characters • easy-to-follow plots • popular topics
For children who are ready to read on their own.

Reading Paragraphs   Grades 2–3
• challenging vocabulary • short paragraphs • exciting stories
For newly independent readers who read simple sentences
with confidence.

Ready for Chapters   Grades 2–4
• chapters • longer paragraphs • full-color art
For children who want to take the plunge into chapter books
but still like colorful pictures.

STEP INTO READING® is designed to give every child a successful
reading experience. The grade levels are only guides; children will progress
through the steps at their own speed, developing confidence in their reading.
The F&P Text Level on the back cover serves as another tool to help you
choose the right book for your child.

Remember, a lifetime love of reading starts with a single step!

In memory of Howard and his '57 Ford tractor
—C.R.

Text copyright © 2021 by Candice Ransom
Cover art and interior illustrations copyright © 2021 by Mike Yamada

All rights reserved.
Published in the United States by Random House Children's Books, a division of
Penguin Random House LLC, New York.

Step into Reading, Random House, and the Random House colophon are registered
trademarks of Penguin Random House LLC.

Visit us on the Web!
StepIntoReading.com
rhcbooks.com

Educators and librarians, for a variety of teaching tools, visit us at RHTeachersLibrarians.com

Library of Congress Cataloging-in-Publication Data
Names: Ransom, Candice F., author. | Yamada, Mike, illustrator.
Title: Go, go, tractors! / by Candice Ransom ; illustrated by Mike Yamada.
Description: First edition. | New York : Random House Children's Books, [2021] |
Series: Step into reading. Step 1 | Audience: Ages 4–6. | Audience: Grades K–1. |
Summary: "A brother and sister explore all the different kinds of tractors there are."
—Provided by publisher.
Identifiers: LCCN 2019051693 (print) | LCCN 2019051694 (ebook) |
ISBN 978-1-9848-5254-0 (trade paperback) | ISBN 978-1-9848-5255-7 (library binding) |
ISBN 978-1-9848-5256-4 (ebook)
Subjects: CYAC: Stories in rhyme. | Tractors—Fiction. | Brothers and sisters—Fiction.
Classification: LCC PZ8.3.R1467 Go 2021 (print) | LCC PZ8.3.R1467 (ebook) | DDC [E]—dc23

Printed in the United States of America
10 9 8 7 6 5 4 3 2 1
First Edition

This book has been officially leveled by using the F&P Text Level Gradient™ Leveling System.

STEP INTO READING®

1
STEP
READY TO READ

GO, GO, TRACTORS!

by Candice Ransom
illustrated by Mike Yamada

Random House 🏠 New York

Tractor here.

Tractor there.

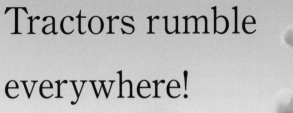

Tractors rumble
everywhere!

Big new tractor

makes neat rows.

Old red tractor
scares off crows!

Yellow tractor

mows the weeds.

Purple tractor
drops the seeds.

Tractors carry,

rake,

and plow.

Look out for the
poky cow!

Muddy hillside.

Wheels must grip.

Steady, tractor!
Do not slip!

Tractors push.

Tractors flash.

Heavy tractors
smash the trash.

Giant tractors,

tall and wide.

Little tractors
we can ride.

Haul the pumpkins.

Pick up hay.

Work is over!

Time to play!

Tractors pull.

Tractors strain.

Tractors tug.

We won!

Hooray!

On the farm.

On the road.

Busy tractors.

Go, go, go!